KU-594-530

MRS PEPPERPOT LEARNS TO SWIM
A RED FOX BOOK 978 1 782 95577 1

First published in Great Britain by Hutchinson,
an imprint of Random House Children's Publishers UK
A Random House Group Company

Hutchinson edition published 1968
This Red Fox edition published 2013

1 3 5 7 9 10 8 6 4 2

Text copyright © Alf Prøysen, 1968
English translation copyright © Hutchinson Children's Books, 1968
Text abridgement copyright © Random House Children's Publishers UK, 2005
Illustrations copyright © Hilda Offen, 2005

The right of Alf Prøysen and Hilda Offen to be identified as the author and illustrator of this work
has been asserted in accordance with the Copyright, Designs and Patents Act 1988.

All rights reserved.

Red Fox Books are published by Random House Children's Publishers UK,
61–63 Uxbridge Road, London W5 5SA

www.**randomhousechildrens**.co.uk
www.**randomhouse**.co.uk

Addresses for companies within The Random House Group Limited can be found at:
www.randomhouse.co.uk/offices.htm

THE RANDOM HOUSE GROUP Limited Reg. No. 954009

A CIP catalogue record for this book is available from the British Library.

Printed in China

Mrs Pepperpot
Learns to Swim

Alf Prøysen ❖ **Hilda Offen**

RED FOX

In the warm weather Mrs Pepperpot always walked through the wood when she went shopping. In the middle of the wood was a large pool where the village children swam. They splashed about and raced each other up and down.

Mrs Pepperpot always stopped to watch and she would sigh to herself and think, If only I could do that! Because nobody had taught her to swim when she was a little girl.

One day when she got home she decided to practise
swimming in the kitchen. She balanced herself
on her tummy on the kitchen stool but when
she flung out her arms, she knocked
a saucepan of soup off the stove!

Every night she would dream about swimming. One night she dreamed she could do the breaststroke. She stretched forward her arms, bent her knees and then – WHAM! – one foot almost kicked a hole in the wall, the other knocked Mr Pepperpot out of bed!

"What's the matter with you?" said Mr Pepperpot.

"I'm swimming," answered Mrs Pepperpot, who was still half in a dream, "and it's the most wonderful feeling!"

"Well, it's not wonderful for me, I can tell you!" said Mr Pepperpot crossly.

Then came a bright, warm day when all the village children were going on a picnic in the mountains.

That's good, thought Mrs Pepperpot. There'll be no children in the pool today and I'll have a chance to learn how to swim. And she walked through the wood to the pool.

It certainly looked inviting, with the sun shining down through the leaves and making pretty patterns on the still water.

She sat down on the soft grass and took off her shoes and stockings. Peering over the edge, she could see the water was very shallow so she stood up and said to herself, "All right, Mrs P, here goes!" And she jumped in.

But just at that moment, she SHRANK!

And now, of course, the pool seemed like an ocean to
the tiny Mrs Pepperpot. "Help, help!" she cried.
"Hold on!" said a deep, throaty voice from below.

And a large frog swam smoothly towards her. "You should NEVER jump in a pool if you don't have someone with you," he said. "Now get on my back." And he swam to a rock so Mrs Pepperpot could get her breath.

"You're a very good swimmer," said Mrs Pepperpot.

The frog puffed himself up importantly. "I'm the best swimming teacher in this pool," he said.

"D'you think you could teach *me* to swim?" asked Mrs Pepperpot.

"Of course. We'll begin right away, if you like. Frogs are very good at breaststroke. You climb on my back and watch what I do."

Mrs Pepperpot watched how the frog moved his arms and legs in time.

Then he found her a little piece of floating wood and told her to hang on. And she pushed along with her legs, just like the frog had done.

After a while she found herself swimming along without the piece of wood.

"Yippee!" she shouted with excitement.

But the frog, who had been swimming close to her all the time, came up behind her and lifted her onto his back. "That's enough for the moment," he said, and took her back to the rock for a rest.

Mrs Pepperpot was feeling so pleased with herself, she wanted to carry straight on and learn the crawl.

"Not so fast, my dear," the frog said. "You must keep practising breaststroke before you can do other things. But I'll get my tadpoles to give you a show of water acrobatics. How's that?"

"Wonderful!" said Mrs Pepperpot.

"Come on, children," he croaked. "I want you to show this lady all your best tricks."

First the tadpoles swam
to the top of the water...

then they dived
to the bottom...

then they wove in and out of the reeds in a beautiful pattern.

And then, like aeroplanes doing acrobatics, they rolled over and over and looped the loop.

The frog had puffed himself up so much
he was nearly bursting with pride.

Mrs Pepperpot was just standing up to cheer the tadpoles when she found herself rolling about in what seemed more like a large puddle than a deep pool; she had GROWN!

As she picked herself up and waded out of the water to the bank she could see no sign of the frog or the tadpoles so she hurried home.

A few days passed before Mrs Pepperpot got a chance to go back to the pool. But before she knew it she was swimming along and she felt very proud.

Then she saw that she was being followed. There was the frog and behind him were all the tadpoles! The frog came to the top of the water and gave a loud croak.

"Thanks, Mr Frog," said Mrs Pepperpot. "You're the best swimming teacher in the world!"

"I told you so!" said the frog.

And with an elegant kick of his back legs, he did a nose-dive down into the pool and all the tadpoles followed after.

MORE MRS PEPPERPOT BOOKS
FOR YOU TO ENJOY!

MRS PEPPERPOT
MINDS THE BABY

A classic story with a
touch of magic

ALF PRØYSEN ❖ HILDA OFFEN

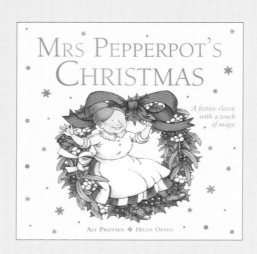

MRS PEPPERPOT'S
CHRISTMAS

A festive classic
with a touch
of magic

ALF PRØYSEN ❖ HILDA OFFEN

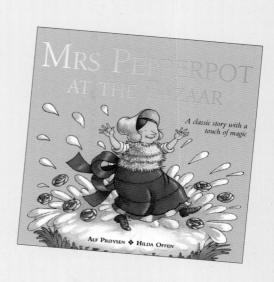

MRS PEPPERPOT
AT THE BAZAAR

A classic story with a
touch of magic

ALF PRØYSEN ❖ HILDA OFFEN

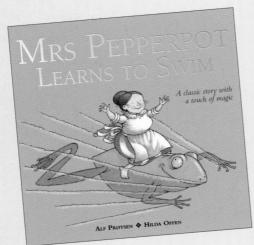

MRS PEPPERPOT
LEARNS TO SWIM

A classic story with
a touch of magic

ALF PRØYSEN ❖ HILDA OFFEN

MRS PEPPERPOT
AND THE
TREASURE

A classic story with a
touch of magic

ALF PRØYSEN ❖ HILDA OFFEN